AF527472

THE SLEEPY PRINCESS

A Tale of Love, Loss, and Light

By
Alice Natures

The Sleepy Princess: A Tale of Love, Loss, and Light

© 2025 Aarti Singh. All rights reserved.

Published by Alice Natures

ISBN: 978-93-5592-465-0

No part of this book may be reproduced, distributed, or transmitted in any form or by any means — electronic or mechanical — including photocopying, recording, or by any information storage and retrieval system, without the prior written permission of the author, except for brief quotations used in reviews or critical articles.

This is a work of fiction. Names, characters, events, and places are products of the author's imagination or used fictitiously. Any resemblance to actual persons, living or dead, or actual events is purely coincidental.

Cover Design and Layout: Alice Natures Studio
Story and Text: Aarti Singh
Edited and Compiled by: Aarti Singh
First Edition — 2025

Printed in India by Amazon KDP

For more works, visit
☛ *alicenatures.blogspot.com*

To the dreamers who still believe in magic and kindness, your heart is your lantern; keep it glowing, and find your way to the love that never fades.

My heartfelt thanks to everyone who believed in The Sleepy Princess, and to all the dreamers who still trust the light within their hearts.

Your warmth, kindness, and faith in small wonders keep stories like this alive.

TABLE OF CONTENTS

PROLOGUE

The Day of Celebration

Once upon a time, in the town of Crystalin, it was a day of celebration and joy. A beautiful little princess was born to King James and Queen Jasmin. The whole town rejoiced with music, dancing, and cheer.

The king and queen named their darling girl Rose, after her rosy cheeks and her gentle face that resembled the beauty and purity of a white rose.

But who knew what the future held, or that their happiness would not last long?

Yet long before the curse was ever spoken, a quieter story had already begun — the tale of a heart once filled with love, slowly shadowed by grief.

Far beyond the castle walls, in the misty woods of Crystalin, another mother watched the lights of the palace and wept.

CHAPTER 1

The Witch's Revenge

In the midst of the celebration, Rose was kidnapped by Rachel, a witch who lived outside the town. Rachel had hated the royal family for over a decade. She had always felt wronged by the townspeople, and when she heard of the princess's birth, she decided to take revenge by stealing their child.

Rachel sneaked into the palace that night, casting a spell of slumber over the entire town. When everyone fell into a deep sleep, she entered the castle and found little Rose lying in her crib.

As Rachel walked toward the baby, she froze. Rose was awake—and smiling at her. That innocent, heart-melting smile stirred something deep inside Rachel. It reminded her of her own little daughter, who had died ten years ago.

CHAPTER 2

Little Sunshine

Rachel had once called her daughter Little Sunshine, for she was the ray of hope and light in her life. But when the child was only five months old, she fell sick and passed away.

Rachel still remembered that terrible day as if it had happened yesterday. Her baby needed urgent care, but Rachel lived deep in the forest. Desperate, she ran toward the town to get a doctor.

It was the annual Establishment Day of Crystalin. Grand celebrations filled the streets, and because of an earlier attack on the king's convoy, the city gates were heavily guarded and closed.

Rachel pleaded and cried for hours at the gate, begging to be let in. The guards refused, saying it was the king's strict order that no one was to enter, no matter the reason.

Just as Rachel was about to lose hope, she saw the town's doctor returning. She ran to him, fell to her knees, and begged for help. Moved by her tears, the doctor agreed to come. Rachel cast a spell to open a magic gate, and in an instant, they were back at her home.

But when they entered the room, everything was silent. Only her pet crow—who could take human form—sat near the crib, tears glistening in his eyes. Rachel rushed to her daughter, but the baby did not move. The doctor bowed his head and whispered, "She's gone."

CHAPTER 3

The Stolen Princess

Back in the present, Rachel's thoughts snapped back as the clock struck the hour. She took little Rose into her arms. Suddenly, the door opened, and Queen Jasmin entered to check on her child as the spell was breaking.

Seeing Rachel holding the princess, Jasmin understood what had happened and ran forward. But in a flash, Rachel cast another spell and vanished into thin air with Rose.

Rachel locked the child in an old house near the river, raising her there. She cared for Rose tenderly for years, for the child reminded her of Little Sunshine—but her heart ached with both love and bitterness.

Years passed. Rose grew into a graceful young woman of eighteen, with shiny black hair, gentle brown eyes, and a warm smile that could melt any heart.

She was raised by the crow, who acted as her guardian, while Rachel visited from time to time. Rose called Rachel Mother, which filled Rachel with both joy and sorrow.

But even love born from loss carries its shadow.

On quiet nights, when the river whispered to the stars, Rachel would hum to herself — a lullaby half-forgotten. Rose, listening through the window, often felt her heart ache, though she never knew why.

Beneath that melody slept an old grief, waiting to wake once more.

CHAPTER 4

The Curse Of Nightmares

One day, while playing near the river, Rose heard Rachel's voice. She smiled mischievously, planning to sneak up and hug her "mother" from behind. But as she crept closer, she overheard Rachel and the crow talking about her kidnapping, Little Sunshine, and what had happened on the day of her birth.

Shocked and heartbroken, Rose ran away from them. Lost in thought, she wandered deep into the forest and didn't realize it was getting dark. She sat beneath a tree and began to cry. Though brave at heart, Rose had feared the night ever since she was twelve.

When she was twelve, she had followed a butterfly into Rachel's room and accidentally broken a framed photo of Little Sunshine. Rachel, waking from rest, saw the shattered frame and was overcome with grief and anger. In a burst of emotion, she cast a spell of sleepless nightmares on Rose.

Terrified, Rose ran outside crying. The crow followed and tried to comfort her.

In the forest, a kind monk found the weeping girl. He gently asked what was wrong, and Rose told him everything—her strange curse, her endless nightmares, and how she longed for peace.

The monk closed his eyes and prayed quietly. When he opened them, he said,

"If you wish to break the curse and return home, follow the floating lanterns in the sky and the flower baskets that drift upon the river. They will guide you."

CHAPTER 5

The Journey Of Lanterns

Every year, near the princess's birthday, the king, queen, and all the townspeople lit sky lanterns and floated flower baskets on the river. They prayed to the gods of the sky and water for Rose's safety and return. A heavenly fairy had once told them to do so when their daughter was taken.

Hearing the monk's words, Rose wiped her tears and decided to follow the lanterns and baskets.

The next day, she began her journey. By day, she followed the flower baskets down the river; by night, the glowing lanterns became her stars of hope. The path was long and difficult, and many times she grew tired or wanted to give up—but her determination to find home kept her moving.

One afternoon, while resting beside the river, Rose saw a bear cub struggling to cross the strong current. She rushed into the water to help, but before she reached him, the cub had already fallen in.

The river was too deep, and the little bear was drowning. Rose swam as fast as she could, but the cub was being pulled away by the current until he got caught in the branches of a fallen tree. Rose reached him just in time, pulled him free, and carried him safely to shore.

The cub began to cry loudly. Rose tried to comfort him, but moments later, a large mother bear came running. Seeing Rose holding her child, the mother bear thought she had harmed him and attacked in rage. Rose stumbled back in fear.

But the little bear quickly ran between them and told his mother what had happened. Realizing the truth, the mother bear apologized and thanked Rose for saving her child. She invited Rose to rest in their cave for the night.

As Rose watched the mother and cub play, her eyes filled with tears. Having never known a mother's love, she whispered, "What is a mother, and what does her love feel like?"

The mother bear noticed her sadness and asked what was wrong. Rose told her everything—her life with Rachel, the curse, and her journey to find home. The kind bear decided to accompany Rose until she reached the edge of her town.

By dawn, the mist lifted and the forest grew thin. The river that had carried her for so long now whispered its farewell, turning toward the fields beyond.

Rose paused and looked back — at the winding waters, the sleeping mountains, and the sky still glowing with the last of the lanterns. For the first time, she felt the world gently guiding her home.

CHAPTER 6

The Return To Crystalin

Meanwhile, in the forest, Rachel searched tirelessly for Rose. She realized only now how deeply she loved the girl. Each day she searched the woods, and each night she studied her magic books, hoping to find a spell that would bring Rose back.

After days of traveling, Rose and the mother bear finally reached the gates of Crystalin. The bear told Rose it was time for her to continue alone, for her journey was complete. They said goodbye with tears and love.

When Rose reached the city gates, the guards refused to let her in, mistaking her for a wanderer. But a passing villager who worked at the palace noticed her necklace—the royal emblem—and recognized her. He rushed to tell the guards, and together they brought Rose to the palace.

The king and queen wept with joy as they embraced their long-lost daughter. Queen Jasmin held Rose in her arms, crying tears of happiness.

Seeing how tired and sleepy her daughter was, the queen brought her food, then took her to the princess's chamber. Rose told her about the nightmares that had haunted her for years. The queen smiled softly and said, "Lie down on my lap, my dear. Close your eyes."

She stroked Rose's hair gently and sang her a soft lullaby.
For the first time in years, Rose fell into a deep, peaceful sleep—without nightmares. The curse was finally broken.

From that day on, Rose lived happily with her family—her father, her mother, and her little sister, Caroline, who had been adopted after Rose's disappearance.

That night, the palace shimmered with lantern light. From her window, Rose could see their golden glow drifting high into the stars — each one a whisper of love, carrying prayers into the night.

As she closed her eyes, her mother's lullaby still echoed softly in her heart. And far away, beyond the hills and rivers, another heart — lonely and worn — felt that same melody reach through the wind.

CHAPTER 7

The Whisper In The Forest

Far away in the forest, Rachel heard the news of Rose's safe return. Exhausted from days of searching, she fell to the ground as tears filled her eyes. Looking up at the night sky, she whispered, "I'm sorry, my child. Have a happy life."

The wind carried her words into the glowing night, where the lanterns floated high above Crystalin—each one a symbol of love, forgiveness, and peace.

EPILOGUE

The Light That Never Sleeps

That night, as the last lantern disappeared into the clouds, the stars above Crystalin shimmered brighter than ever before.

And though many years passed, whenever the townspeople released their lanterns, they believed they saw one glowing lantern in the shape of a rose—drifting higher than all the rest.

They said it was the light of a love that never fades, a love that finally found its way home.

AUTHOR'S NOTE

I wrote The Sleepy Princess during a time when I was learning how love, loss, and even hate can live together in the same heart. Every word became a way to understand how light survives even through the darkest nights.

This story is also about a mother's love — endless and unconditional, even when hidden behind mistakes, pain, or distance. It reminds us that not everything in life is simply white or black. Sometimes, we just don't know the other side of the story. Sometimes, even those who seem lost, broken, or drawn toward darkness are only grieving — trying to find their way back to love and hope.

The story also reminds us that we often realize the value of what truly matters only when we lose it — and through that ache, we learn what love really means.

I hope this story reaches you on a quiet evening and reminds you that light, kindness, and forgiveness always find their way home.

With love and gratitude,
— Alice Natures

About the Author

Alice Natures is the creative name of writer and artist Aarti Singh, who believes in the quiet power of words and the beauty found in small, mindful moments.

Her work flows across age groups and themes — from self-love journals and creative reflections to gentle stories and coloring books — all created with one simple intention: to help others reconnect with themselves and find light in softness.

The Sleepy Princess: A Tale of Love, Loss, and Light is her debut story, inspired by her belief that even in darkness, love and forgiveness can bloom.

When she isn't writing, Aarti enjoys quiet mornings with tea, exploring nature-inspired ideas, and curating calm, creative spaces that spark hope and kindness.

Learn more at

alicenatures.blogspot.com

www.ingramcontent.com/pod-product-compliance
Ingram Content Group UK Ltd.
Pitfield, Milton Keynes, MK11 3LW, UK
UKHW061436190726
13845UKWH00023B/183
* 9 7 8 9 3 5 5 9 2 4 6 5 0 *